THE LE
SPARKHILL

GW00818632

First published by Fairfield Books in 2022

fairfield books

Fairfield Books
Bedser Stand, Kia Oval
London, SE11 5SS

Typeset in Garamond
Typesetting by Rob Whitehouse
Illustrations by Jen Khatun

All rights reserved. No part of this book may be reproduced,
sold, utilised or transmitted in any form or by any electronic
or mechanical means, including photocopying, recording
or by any information storage and retrieval system, without
prior permission in writing from the publishers

The views and opinions expressed in this book are those of the
authors and do not necessarily reflect the views of the publishers

© 2022 Moeen Ali and Tanya Aldred
ISBN 978-1-915237-08-8

A CIP catalogue record for is available from the British Library

Printed by CPI Group (UK)

THE LEGEND OF SPARKHILL

by Moeen Ali OBE
and Tanya Aldred

illustrated by Jen Khatun

Chapter 1

The noise was wild, disorderly. With just one ball left of the World Cup final, England needed five runs to win. Mo stood in the middle of the pitch as Jos Buttler whispered in his ear: "If anyone can do it, it's you." Mo shook his head modestly and wandered back to the stumps. He tapped his bat twice on the ground and watched as Pat Cummins sprinted in: it was going to be a bouncer, he knew it would be a bouncer...

"Mo Aqeel." Mo snapped back to reality. "Are you listening?" Ah. School. He nodded his head at Miss Joseph and tried to look interested. He glanced at the board and narrowed his eyes.

Trigonometry. Some teachers had a very weird sense of humour.

Outside, the rain continued to pour down. That meant one thing: no cricket. Mo screwed the point of his pencil into his maths book. No cricket – no nets. No nets – no batting. No batting – no scoop shot. No scoop – no selection. No scouting. No first game for Warwickshire, no smart blue cap emblazoned with the Warwickshire bear. No England phone call. He'd never nod at his reflection in the dressing-room mirror before clomping down through the Long Room at Lord's in his spikes, as the old men in blazers applauded him. Everything was ruined. Snap! Now his pencil had gone too.

He looked outside again. Then he glanced at the clock – how could it possibly take so long for a hand to TICK DOWN THE MINUTES?

* * *

The final bell rang. Mo and his best friend Sammy charged out of school and walked through the sodden park. Water dripped down from the trees onto the basketball courts where they liked to hang out on drier days. They said goodbye at the busy high street, and Mo trudged on till he came to Sparkhill Avenue, a road of identical terraced houses. There he bumped into his little brother Hassan, who had run ahead of Mum to try and beat Mo home from school.

Mo and Hassan opened the door of number 21 and jostled each other to be first through the door. Dad, known to everyone as Big M, was on the sofa, watching a rerun of an old IPL final on TV. Big M wasn't really very big, only a handy five foot 7 in his bare feet, and perhaps a little rounder across the middle than in his prime.

"Hello boys!"

Mo kicked his bag across the room. "It's raining," he said, by way of a greeting. "No cricket tonight."

Big M leaned back and looked at him. "Pick your bag up Mo," he said. "The thing is, what you need is a good temperament. Get one of those and you can take on the world."

Mo sighed and sunk into the sofa. Dad got up and brought in some samosas from the kitchen. Mo grabbed one, the warm flaky pastry melting on his tongue, and took a last look out of the window – the rain fell fatly into the puddles forming in the potholes on the road. Practice would have to wait for another day.

Chapter 2

Mo woke on Sunday morning to sunlight squeezing through the curtains of the room he shared with Hassan. The curtains had cars on them – perhaps not what a 12-year-old would choose, but Hassan liked them and Mo could live with that.

He looked over at his brother, who was snoring with his mouth open. Mo squeezed the foam ball he was holding and thought about lobbing it into Hassan's mouth, but instead he threw himself a few catches against the sloping roof, got up, squeezed between the beds and went downstairs for breakfast.

Mum was in the kitchen. She looked tired, her long dark hair tied back in a plait, a strip of grey that they affectionately called her badger stripe stretching from her centre parting to her left ear. Mo gave her a hug and swiped a piece of toast off the breakfast table.

"Sit down when you're eating Mo," she said. And she put down her knife and stopped chopping carrots and potatoes for the bubbling pot on the stove. She handed Mo a cup of tea and gave him a look. Mo knew what it meant. He suddenly became very interested in pouring himself some cornflakes.

"Have you started your homework?"

Mo sighed.

He'd been in a bit of trouble the previous term at school. He knew it. Mum knew it. Slacking in his lessons, some backchat, just a bit of a laugh really, but the teachers hadn't seen it like that. He'd even been suspended for a few days – and Mum and Dad were onto him now. School-obsessed, checking the homework website, refusing to let him do anything, even 20 minutes on the X-box, until everything was done.

"Mo, are you listening?"

But Mo had sensed someone looking at him – he glanced up. It was Hassan, standing in the doorway in his pyjamas. His hair, which was stupidly long, was hanging over his face but he was unmistakably laughing.

Mo launched at him, just catching Hassan's legs with his fingertips, not enough to hurt him, but hard enough for Hassan to dive theatrically onto the kitchen floor, clutching his thigh as if in extreme agony.

"Can you two just cut it out?" said Mum. "You've got two hours before cricket practice, you've both got homework to do and I want to cook dinner before going to work." Mum worked at the local retirement home, helping the old people get up, eat and go to the toilet. Mo didn't fancy it much but he'd seen Mum at work and knew she was brilliant – kind and patient.

Mo muttered something to Hassan, and gave him a quick kick to his ankle for good measure. Then he finished his cornflakes and dug around in his school bag.

He hated maths. What use was it? Why, when he was going to be a professional cricketer, did he need to know the value of x? Did Joe Root do algebra in the dressing-room? Did Babar Azam talk about trigonometry in interviews?

But Dad would be here soon, and if he hadn't done his homework, Dad wouldn't take him to cricket training. Dad would check and Dad would know. He pulled his protractor out of his pencil case and opened his books.

HassAN

Chapter 3

They arrived at Sparkhill Cricket Club early. Four of them squeezed onto the back seat – Mo and Hassan and their cousins Rayaan and Aamir – and Dad and Uncle Bilal in the front chatting about Pakistan's fortunes. In the back, the talk was all about the upcoming game against Fenchurch in the cup semi-final.

Fenchurch were their local rivals from the other side of town. A bigger club, a wealthier club, with a flashy clubhouse and tennis courts on the side. The team were always well-turned out, in matching maroon caps and smart training tops with names on the back.

Sparkhill's ground was surrounded on all sides by houses. Some had garden gates that opened almost straight onto the boundary rope – it was Mo's dream to live so close to the cricket.

Mike Collins was the man in charge. He did everything. He mowed the grass, he manned the bar, he ran the local quiz night. He could be a bit gruff, but Dad always said he had a heart of gold. Whatever that meant.

Mo, Hassan, Rayaan and Aamir jumped out of the beat-up Vauxhall that Bilal was so proud of. "Could do with a clean," Mo shouted as he slammed the boot and scarpered with his kit bag before Bilal could reach him.

Mike immediately sent them running around the boundary. Mo was first back – he was pretty fit from all the football he played. Football was his second love, Liverpool Football Club to be exact. He'd had trials with West Brom last year but it hadn't worked out. He told his friends that it was because the coach didn't like him, but the real reason was that the other boys were more skilful. And sometimes that was just the way it was.

Cricket, however, was something else. He was good at cricket, really good. Everyone told him that, but more than that he just knew. He knew how to send a ball pinging off the bat. He knew how to time a cover-drive so it beat the most athletic fielder. And he had a kind of sixth sense about where the bowler was going to land the ball. A left-hander with a keen sense of timing – England were always in the market for a guy like him, especially with his off-breaks to throw into the mix too.

SAMMY

Ok, there wasn't much of him yet. He was short and scrawny – Mum was always trying to get him to eat more but he never seemed to grow any taller. Dad was always telling him not to worry but, looking at Dad, he didn't find that very reassuring.

Mike divided them into groups. Mo went with the Under-13s. He always played up an age-group, as did Sammy and Aisha. Sammy not only went to school with Mo, they hung round together after school too – always running, never stopping. Sammy was a big-hitting batter, nearly a foot taller than Mo, and he loved to hit fast bowlers back over their heads. More importantly he always had a big smile on his face. When Mo got angry, Sammy calmed him down. When Mo got mad, Sammy held him back. And when Mo got too big for his boots, Sammy laughed at him.

And then there was Aisha. Aisha was petite but fast with short shiny black hair. She had quietly forced her way into the side simply by being very good, a wily bowler and a clever batter.

He would never admit it to her face – she was sure enough of herself already – but Mo admired

Aisha

Aisha a lot. She didn't care what other people thought, really didn't care. She could be blunt, but she was never unkind. Aisha, Sammy and Mo – they were a formidable team.

Mike sent them over to the nets, where they took it in turns to bowl and have a bat. Mo's off-breaks were coming out ok, loopy but with a bit of fizz. Sammy blundered down the pitch and tried to hit him into the branches of the conker tree on the far side of the ground. Twice Mo got him out, once knocking out his stumps, once catching him off

14

his own bowling. Sammy pulled off his helmet. "Lucky!" he said.

When they were finished, they gathered round Mike. "Right Under-13s, he said. "We've got a week until the semi-final against Fenchurch." He paused so everyone could boo. "So this week I want you to think about cricket and only cricket. You think cricket, you drink cricket and you sleep cricket. We're going to have our usual Wednesday practice and an extra practice on Thursday because you lot need all the help you can get. If you don't turn up, you won't be picked. No excuses."

Mo looked at Aisha and pulled a face. She gave him a sympathetic squeeze of the arm. She knew what he knew, that Thursday night in the Aqeel household meant Arabic class at the mosque. Mum and Dad weren't strict Muslims, but that was compulsory.

He didn't mind it actually, most of the time. He liked the way the words sounded, rolling off his tongue. He liked praying too, clearing his mind from whatever had got to him during the day.

But if cricket clashed with Arabic class – or anything else – there was just no contest. Mo always wanted to be on the cricket field. One of the reasons he'd joined Sparkhill CC was that they practised on Wednesdays or Sundays, never Thursdays.

He'd just have to persuade Mum and Dad to let him off this week.

Chapter 4

That evening, Mo cleared up everyone's dinner without being asked. He scraped the food from the plates into the compost bin, even the bits of cauliflower Hassan had tried to hide.

Then he got his homework out with a flourish and did his English and his geography very publicly. He saw Mum raising her eyebrows but pretended not to see.

After completing all his homework without a murmur, he played a game of chess with Hassan, letting him win. Next he put all his clean clothes away before changing the sheets on both beds.

Surely that was enough? He ran a hand through his hair to flatten it down and went downstairs to where Mum and Dad were having a cup of tea. He sat down.

"How has your day been?"

They looked at him, quizzically. "Very nice thank you Mo," said Mum. "We've noticed how helpful you've been around the house since you came home," said Dad. "It's great to see – keep it up," Then he put his cup down and stood up.

"No!" said Mo. "Wait, I mean. Can I talk to you?"

Dad put the cup down and pulled his chair back in. They both looked at him expectantly.

Mo explained what had happened at cricket and the extra practice before the all-important semi-final next week. "It will just be a one-off," he pleaded. "I'll never ask for a day off Arabic class again."

Dad sighed. Mum looked him in the eye. "I know how important cricket is to you, love, but we don't ask very much from you. All we ask is that you work hard, are a good boy and go to your lessons."

"I know, but…"

"No buts, I'm sorry. You can play every other day of the week but not on a Thursday night."

"Dad?" Mo tried to catch his dad's eye, but Dad was looking at the ground. Mo was disappointed, Dad was as obsessed with cricket as he was – more even – he knew how much Mo wanted to be in the team. He knew how good he was – or could be.

Mo's temper rushed up his spine and exploded out of his mouth. "It doesn't matter what I do. How much homework I finish. How much I do around the house. You're just so selfish, you never listen."

And with that he threw back his chair and stormed out of the room and up the stairs, stamping so hard that the steps wobbled under his feet.

As he climbed, he heard Dad say to his mum, "Don't you think you were a little tough on him?"

But he wasn't going to stick around to hear the end of that conversation. He charged into his room and slammed the door shut. Hassan looked up from his copy of *Match of the Day* magazine. "And you can shut up as well," Mo shouted at him, climbing into bed fully clothed and pulling the duvet over his head. It was dark under there and his head was throbbing, but no-one could see as hot tears of disappointment dripped down his face.

Life just wasn't fair.

Chapter 5

It was Monday lunchtime and Sammy and Mo were lobbing a ball to each other in the playground. They'd already eaten and there was time to kill before lessons restarted. It was warm and they'd taken off their blazers. The cuffs on Sammy's shirts were still done up and his tie hung straight down from his neck, far enough to tuck into his trousers – though even Sammy wouldn't do that. At least, Mo didn't think Sammy would do that. Mo's tie was short and fat, with a deliberately big knot, and he'd loosened his buttons and rolled up his sleeves.

Sammy lobbed a catch high to Mo's right and Mo reached for it with his fingertips but couldn't quite hold on. Sammy said nothing but the sides of his mouth twitched.

Wordlessly Mo threw the ball hard at Sammy's head. Sammy stuck out his huge left paw to parry it and the ball stuck fast. He turned and flicked one high. Mo was quick to react, leaping hare-like and catching it with both hands.

Sammy was bouncing on his toes now. He was so tall and his limbs were so long that it was almost impossible to pass him. Mo chucked the ball to Sammy's right, as hard as he could, to tempt him into a dive, but Sammy had seen the state of the concrete and chose instead to ignore the ball as it flew past him and hit a group of year 7 girls chatting in the sun.

That caused quite a commotion. Mo spotted Mina, who'd been at primary school with him. The boys looked at each other. Where was Aisha when you needed her? With false bravado, Mo strode over to retrieve the ball, before the pair of them skulked off to the far end of the playground.

"Well," said Sammy, hopping from foot to foot. "What are you going to do about Thursday?"

"What do you mean? I can't go. Mum and Dad have said so."

"There must be a way, surely."

Mo spun the ball from hand to hand, thinking. He couldn't see a way out. If he wanted to play in the game, he had to go to the Thursday practice. But he couldn't go, because he had to go to Arabic class. Unless...

He turned to Sammy, his brain whirring. "Rayaan," he said.

"You what?"

Rayaan was Mo's oldest cousin, 15 now and an excellent cricketer. The pair of them got on well, they'd got into a few scrapes together over the years. Rayaan had been a bit of a tearaway, but had knuckled down this year with GCSEs to do. Mo had seen him in the library earlier.

"Wait here," he told Sammy, and sprinted into school and up to the first floor.

He found Rayaan slumped in a comfortable chair, gazing blankly at his physics book. He was very happy to be interrupted.

Soooo... this was how it would work. On Thursday, Rayaan would call for Mo and suggest that he was old enough now to walk to the mosque for class with his older cousin. Then, with mum's blessing, they would head off together like good boys except just before they arrived,

Mo would chuck a right turn, disappear into the park to meet Sammy and they'd run to practice together. Afterwards, he'd run back to the park where Rayaan would pick him up, and then they'd calmly walk home, with Rayaan briefing him on the way about anything he should know. And then they'd ring the front door bell. Just like that. No-one need know.

"You're playing with fire, man."

"Come on Rayaan, please."

Rayaan put his book down and looked at Mo. "You want this that badly?"

Mo nodded.

"Ok," said Rayaan, "I'll do it, but don't get caught. Your mum will kill me."

Chapter 6

The days passed in a blur of lessons and sport. After school on Thursday Mo didn't go to the park with his friends, but came straight home, shoved his tracksuit in a bag and hid it behind a bin by the front door. Then he showered and got changed into a smart shirt and trousers. He was just eating dinner when the doorbell rang.

Mo let Dad open it – it was Rayaan. Mo held his breath as he heard them talking on the doorstep, then they both came into the kitchen. Dad had his hand on Rayaan's shoulder.

"Rayaan would like to take Mo to class today," said Dad. Mum looked surprised, then pleased.

"How do you feel about that Mo, would you like to go with your cousin?"

Mo nodded. Mum smiled. "How grown up you're getting," she said and came round the table, gave him a hug and tried to mess with his hair.

"Mum!" he complained, gently batting her off and shovelling down his last bit of dinner. As they walked out Dad shouted: "Behave yourselves." They closed the door slowly behind them. Mo picked up his bag of cricket clothes and they walked on.

After ten minutes they reached the park. "Text me," hissed Rayaan out of the side of his mouth. Mo nodded and dropped back, diving in through the gates as Rayaan walked by. Sammy was waiting for him on a bench. Mo scuttled into the bushes to change and then the two of them ran up the summer streets to the club, keeping pace with each other the whole time. It felt good to be stretching out, and rather thrilling that Mum and Dad didn't know.

Mike was already at the club when they arrived. "Great to see you boys," he said, before sending them over to the nets with the balls, cones and stumps.

It was a good session. Mo had to borrow some kit but he had a long bat and the bowlers gave him a total work-out – bouncers, off-cutters, in-swingers, leg-breaks. Then he worked on his scoop shot – stay dead still, then weight onto the back foot, keep control of the bat angle… again and again he tried it, and again and again he threw his head back in frustration.

Out in the middle, Mike had set up some fielding drills. The idea was that you had to pick the ball up on the run and throw down a single stump. On that single stump was a fifty pence piece. Mo had never seen a group of kids work so hard for 50p. They ran in for 20 minutes but not one of them managed to win the money. "And that," said Mike, pocketing his 50p, "is why you need to be here. You won't be winning any cup, if 15 of you combined can't knock down a stump."

"That was tough," said Aisha, as she, Sammy and Mo walked slowly back to the clubhouse. The boys nodded, their shirts sticking to their backs. Mike had worked them hard today – but if they wanted to beat Fenchurch, that was what they were going to have to do. They bought an orange squash at the bar and sat out in the evening sun, Sammy and Aisha rolling their trouser legs up to their knees to get a tan. "Keep trying," Mo said. Aisha nudged him hard in the ribs.

"Sorry, not sorry. Anyway, you guys better get going," she said, looking at her watch, grabbing her bike from against the wall and hauling her cricket bag onto her back. "Good luck."

As she cycled off, Sammy and Mo started the long run back, taking care to avoid the roads where friends of their parents lived. In the park, Mo changed back, texted Rayaan, who was waiting outside the mosque, and the two of them walked home.

"Enjoy yourself?" called Mum from the sitting room as he walked through the door, his bag of sports stuff stuffed back behind the bin to be picked up later.

"Yes," he said, "Rayaan and his friends were cool, they looked after me. It was great."

"Fabulous!" said Mum and gave him a hug and a cup of tea to take up to bed. Mo hugged her back, feeling a bit guilty. But not too guilty. He tip-toed into his room, careful not to wake the sleeping Hassan. He was so cute when he was asleep. Mo pushed the hair out of his eyes affectionately; Hassan snorted and turned over.

Chapter 7

Sunday came and Dad borrowed Bilal's car to drive to the club. He was an early riser by nature, and cheerfully sang along to the radio as they drove along. "Ooh, look what you made me do," he bellowed, nodding his head along to the beat.

Mo smirked but then in the distance he saw Mina and her friend, walking a dog. Mo's hand quickly went to the volume button to mute it. "Hey," said Dad, "I'm enjoying that."

Dad turned the volume up higher and carried on singing. With increasing desperation, Mo tried to close the window, but it was stuck. Worse still, the lights ahead turned red and Dad ground to a halt, just as the girls walked past.

They looked curiously through the window to where Dad was still doing an appalling version of Taylor Swift. "Hi Mo," Mina called. Then, as the lights turned green and Dad started pulling away, "Nice singing by the way." Mo watched through the rear-view mirror as the girls had a good laugh.

"Friendly," said Dad, glancing at Mo. Mo just shook his head and slunk into the seat. Please let the day get better than this.

Sammy and Aisha were waiting as Mo stomped towards them dragging his bag. "My dad is such an idiot," he muttered as he dumped his kit at their feet.

They started their warm-up, jogging round the pitch. Aisha laughed. "That's nothing," she said. "My dad came to collect me from school wearing a T-shirt saying *I'm with Stupid*. Your dad's nice. Anyway," she stopped running and put her hands on her hips, "Why do you care so much what Mina thinks?" Mo put on a turn of speed that left her far behind.

The rest of the team soon arrived and so did Fenchurch. They were easy to spot, their parents drove shiny BMWs and top-of-the-range Audis. Mike gathered Sparkhill together in the dressing-room, Aisha slid in late after changing in the girls' toilets.

"You may be a rag-tag bunch," started Mike with his usual tact, "but you can take on this lot. Fenchurch, they've got all the gear but… no idea…". The Under-13s groaned.

"But don't underestimate them. Watch the ball, play each on its merit." He paused, hands on his hips. "Fazal's not here, he's hurt his leg falling off a ladder, the buffoon. Where's my twelfth man?" Kamran, a tiny boy with glasses and a crew cut, raised his hand. "Ah, Kamran, you're playing, congratulations. Mo – I want you to be captain. Right. Good luck. Off you go."

He walked blinking into the sunlight. On the one hand they were without the reassuring presence of Fazal; on the other, he, Mo, was captain! In their most important match of the year.

"Well done mate," said Sammy. "You've earned that."

Mo was delighted – he and Dad and Hassan were always talking about tactics and analysing what they heard on the radio and saw on the TV. Dad had made him think more deeply about the game, and how it was easy to criticise captains even though you never really knew what was happening out on the field. Tactics were easy if you were working with robots, Dad said, but captains had to deal with real human beings. And they were way more unreliable.

Mo went up to the Fenchurch coach and asked if they were ready to toss up. The coach was dressed very smartly in a matching tracksuit and box fresh trainers. "Ah, hang about young man, the captain will be along in a minute."

Mo waited. Tightened the laces on his boots, and waited a bit more. Ten minutes went by and the Fenchurch captain still hadn't arrived. The coach was looking at his watch, flustered. He beckoned over a blond-haired kid, who smiled at Mo and introduced himself as Jerome. They were just about to walk out into the middle with the umpires when they heard a shout and a familiar figure ran towards them, rudely pushing Jerome out of the way with the words, "I think you'll find I'm the captain."

Mo couldn't believe his eyes. It was Sluggy Stevens. Last year he'd been playing for Sparkhill, and had even been picked to play for Warwickshire's youth side, but then he'd disappeared over the winter and no-one knew where he'd got to.

He glared at Mo. The two of them had never got on. Mo considered him a bully, who had picked on Aisha. Stevens was a wonderful bowler though, fast and terrifying. The umpires ushered them out to the middle to toss the coin. Stevens was behaving very oddly, sniffing the air, and then wrinkling his nose as if there was a bad smell.

"Heads or tails, gentlemen?" said the umpire.
"Heads," said Mo. It was tails. Stevens chose to
bowl and marched off to put on his spikes.

Chapter 8

The team sat down to watch as Sammy and little Kamran walked out to bat, a double-decker bus and a mini trundling out to the middle. Mo was nervous. He was padded up and ready to go at No.4, but hoping that he wouldn't have to bat for a while.

If these two could just see off Stevens' opening spell... Cup games were twenty overs a side, with bowlers having a maximum of four overs each. Stevens took the ball and started repositioning the field that the coach had spent the last few minutes putting in place. Mo felt for him. Stevens took orders from no-one but himself.

Stevens walked to the top of his run. He had tucked in his shirt and from the back he looked like a man – all big bottom and broad back. He started his run-up, ten quick paces, then a leap and... wham, the ball was down the other end. Sammy stood stock still, his bat playing a shot into the covers long after the ball had passed. But Mo knew he hadn't seen it. Stevens was too quick for Sammy. He couldn't get a bat to the next ball either. Or the one after. It was demoralising for the team – usually Sammy slogged people out of the attack. He lasted until the final ball of the over, when Stevens unleashed a rapid yorker that demolished his stumps.

Stevens roared down the pitch, banging his chest like Tarzan – Mo shook his head. He looked ridiculous. As Stumpy nervously walked out, Sammy returned. "He's faster than ever!" he said, pulling off his helmet and wiping the sweat out of his eyes. "And stupider," said Aisha practising her hook shot.

The bowler at the far end was much smaller, but with the longest run-up Mo had ever seen. Back

he went from the crease. 20, 30, steps away, until he was almost next to the boundary rope. Then he sprinted in, feet flying over the grass, till he slowed down almost completely to deliver the ball. Kamran flicked him off his toes and down to the boundary for four. They were off.

Stumpy and Kamran put on 30 before Stumpy was hit on the pad in front of his stumps and was out lbw. Mo took a deep breath and walked into the middle. As he did, he heard Stevens muttering at mid-off.

Mo ignored him and strode on, sizing up the situation. Stevens had finished his spell and the current bowler was a medium-pacer.

He walked up the pitch to Kamran. "This guy doesn't seem too threatening?"

"He bowls on a length," said Kamran, "but doesn't move it much."

Mo watched as the first ball passed harmlessly by outside off stump. They batted on, steadily building the score, passing 80 before they fell in consecutive balls – Kamran for a steady 40 and Mo for a more flighty 38. The middle-order had a slog before Stevens got two more wickets in his final over. Sparkhill had made 110. Not bad, but not earth-shattering.

Fenchurch made a good start as Ben and Hamza struggled with their lines. Mo brought Aisha on as first change to try and gain some control but it wasn't working. From his position at slip, Mo could see Aisha getting more and more annoyed with herself as the ball wasn't coming out of her hand as smoothly as usual. He could see that she was struggling with her run-up so decided to have a word. It was a risky strategy.

"Um," he started. "Yes," she hissed at him, eyes flaming. He tried again. "I wondered whether you should just try and make things simpler. Forget about the long run-up and go back to four or five paces. I thought that might make things easier." She stared at him. "You thought wrong."

Mo ambled back to stand next to the wicket-keeper Stan. Dad was right, it was way easier talking to a phone than a human. He crouched down and waited for Aisha to walk back to her mark.

Unbelievably she seemed to have listened to him. She turned, almost walked in, and bowled an off-cutter right in the zone. Mo gave her a thumbs-up sign; she ignored him. Two balls later she had a wicket, as the Fenchurch No.2 slashed at a wide one and Stan took the ball comfortably at knee height.

She took two more quick wickets and Sparkhill were up and running. After 15 overs, Fenchurch were 80 for six – scoring quickly enough but with more than half the team out.

Mo called the team together. "Great stuff, but we mustn't be too confident. They're still dangerous. We need to keep the rate down so that they start to panic. I'm going to try spin for a couple of overs."

Mo took the ball in his hand and spun it from right to left. It felt huge.

His first few deliveries came out alright, and the batter couldn't pierce the field. He walked back to the top of his run. Ok, how about something different? He ran his fingers along the seam to rip out the biggest off-break he could manage. The batter pushed forward too hard and the ball flew into Mo's hands… and out again. Mo could hear groans from the slip fielders. Before he knew it, Sammy was at his shoulder. "Keep it together Mo," he said. "We need you."

Wickets fell steadily but still the runs came until, with one over to go, Fenchurch needed eight to win. Their No.11 was Sluggy Stevens – not the greatest stylist but a decent slogger. Mo handed the ball to Aisha. "Keep it tight," he said. She smiled grimly and walked back to her mark.

The first ball was on the button. The second was quite wide and Stevens hit at it wildly, the ball flying over third man and down to the boundary. Aisha ran in again, fractionally wider, and Stevens slashed at it. Mo watched the ball loop, as if in slow motion, from the edge of the bat high to his right and, without thinking about it, he took off. The ball flew into his hand and, milliseconds later as he landed on the ground with a crunch, it was still there.

"YES!!!" Aisha was hurtling towards him. They'd won! They were through to the final! Mo smiled the broadest of smiles.

Moments later he spotted Stevens walking slowly off the pitch and ran up to him, his hand outstretched.

"Hey, bad luck. No hard feelings – you bowled really well."

Stevens turned. "Sparkhill stinks and most of you aren't even English. You're a bunch of losers."

Mo looked at him in disbelief, pulled his hand away and stalked off.

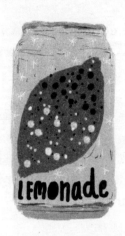

Chapter 9

He walked blankly past his cheering teammates, past Mike, past Dad and straight into the dressing-room before anyone could see the tears. He wiped them away as fast as he could. Idiot tears. Idiot Stevens.

Mo felt completely deflated. What did it matter how well you played, when there were people like that around. People who only saw your skin colour and judged you on that. He was fed up of it. He'd seen it happen too many times, Mum being laughed at in the supermarket because of her accent. People calling Dad names because of his beard.

He heard the dressing-room door being thrown open and looked up to see Mike. The coach didn't bother with small talk.

"How dare you not shake hands at the end of a game? If there is one thing I've told you it is to have respect for the opposition. We'd won the game, you'd led brilliantly, why couldn't you show them a bit of respect?"

Mo stared at him. Did Mike really think he was like that?

He tried to say something but he couldn't get the words out. Mike was ranting now, his cheeks red with anger, his arms flailing about all over the place.

"It is shameful for Sparkhill. We may not be the richest club, but we do things the right way."

There was a knock at the dressing-room door.

"What?" roared Mike.

A small blond head poked round the door. It was Jerome, the boy from Fenchurch who had been going to stand in for Stevens earlier.

"Can't you see we're talking?"

"I know, but..." Mo saw Jerome pull himself up to his full height and take a deep breath. "I think, Sir, there is something you should know."

Mo saw that Mike had responded well to the Sir. He shut up.

"I came to say that I was standing just behind Mo at the end of the game," said Jerome hastily. "I heard what Stevens said to him. It was horrible and racist and I just came to apologise on behalf of the rest of the team."

Mike paused, and turned to look at Mo. "Is this true?"

Mo nodded, tears still smarting his eyes.

Mike thanked Jerome and stalked out of the door.

Jerome inched further into the room and sat down beside Mo. "Sorry," he said. Then he coughed. "But congratulations – you're into the final!" He pulled out a can of lemonade from his pocket. "Here, do you want some?" Mo thanked him, flicked open the can and took a long swig. He felt the bubbles float down into his stomach – and he turned to Jerome and smiled.

In the car home, they were quiet. Dad turned the radio on and they listened to the Test match, where England were struggling. As he parked the car outside Bilal's house, Dad switched the radio off and turned to Mo.

"Hey Mo, well played today."

"Thanks Dad."

"You led the team with real skill and you batted like Saeed Anwar himself, all wrist and style. Then he paused. "But the other stuff…"

Mo looked down. He really didn't want to talk about it.

Dad cleared his throat. "When you go through life you'll meet people who don't like you because of where you're from, or where your parents are from, or your accent, or the colour of your skin, or the god that you believe in.

"The problem is with them, not with you. All you can do is behave like a decent human being." He sighed.

"I know it can be tough, son. Believe me, I've been there." He put his hand on Mo's shoulder. "Come on, let's go home. If Mum's back from work, we'll get a takeaway to celebrate."

Chapter 10

The next few weeks passed quickly. There were end-of-term exams – in which he did ok, and surprisingly well in English, which pleased Mum no end. And then there was sports day, where he won the 100 metres and Sammy won the javelin.

As the teachers started to relax, year 7 spent the last couple of weeks watching DVDs and doing quizzes. It was one of those warm Julys where the sun never seemed to go down and the air was rich with grass cuttings and anticipation.

After school they wandered off to the park and played cricket, and more cricket, in the enclosed courts nearby, until the older boys shoved them off to play basketball at about six o'clock. Mo didn't mind that – when it got late, when large groups gathered, when there was a smell of danger, it was good to be inside with Hassan playing corridor cricket or on the X-box.

After school broke up, Dad took some time off to entertain the boys. He wanted them outside doing something. Cricket mostly.

Hassan moaned sometimes. He liked lounging around, but it was fine by Mo. Dad would pack up the kit bags and take Mo, Hassan and sometimes Bilal's boys to the club. Dad would spend hours bowling at them, trying to get them fluent. Front foot, back foot, drive, cut – he'd give instructions before he bowled. Mo and Hassan sometimes had a quiet laugh at him, this small, bearded man in sandals shouting at them from the shadows.

One thing Dad wouldn't teach Mo was the scoop shot. He said he didn't need it. That Mo should master all the other shots first, the classical ones. He needed to drive and cut and pull and hook and defend on the front and back foot. Then he could experiment.

Sometimes when they were tired they'd sit and watch Rayaan, who was going for trials with Warwickshire, and eat their picnic – cheese sandwiches, samosas, apples, biscuits.

Mo loved these summer days, long hours spent at the club, chewing the fat with Bilal, Dad, Mum when she was back from work, his cousins, Sammy and Aisha. He didn't mind that they couldn't afford to go on holiday.

What's more, he had something to work towards: the final. It was supposed to have been held at the end of term but had been postponed to the end of the summer holidays. They were going to play Greystone CC, a new club and one Sparkhill hadn't played before. But a glance at their results was worrying – they'd crushed most of their opponents this season.

Chapter 11

With two weeks of the holiday left, and two weeks until the final, Mike stepped up the pressure. Practice was going to be two hours instead of one and half, and they'd be netting on a Thursday as well.

Sammy suggested to Mo that he talk to Mike about it, explain the situation – but Mo didn't want any favours, or anyone to judge him or his family. He was going to have to depend on Rayaan again.

Rayaan was not keen. "Mo – I don't want to lie to your mum and dad, they're like second parents to me. Auntie would be really upset."

"Just twice more," Mo pleaded, "that'll be it, then it's the end of the season. They won't find out. And it's not like I'm going out drinking or smoking – I'm playing cricket."

So Rayaan agreed – twice more and twice more only – and Mo and Sammy and Aisha and the rest of the team spent consecutive Thursday nights up at the club practising everything and anything – run outs, slip catching, endless forward defences. Mike worked them till their thighs ached and their hands stung. It was nearly 8.30 when Mike called time on the final practice session before the match. "We're going to keep the same team as for the semi-final," he told them. "Fazal is only just back up and running so we don't want to risk him. Mo – you'll be captain again. Now sleep well everybody, and I'll see you here bright and early on Sunday morning. Off you go."

Sammy and Mo ran back slowly, dissecting the session. As they reached the entrance to the park, a car slowed down to let them cross the road. Mo locked eyes with the driver to say thank you. It was Dad's friend Dave, and sitting in the passenger seat next to him was Uncle Bilal.

Chapter 12

Mo and Sammy stood in the park staring at each other.

"Are you sure that was Bilal?"

"I'm sure that was Bilal."

"Ah."

"Yeah." Mo put his head in his hands. "I'm in deep trouble. I'm in really deep trouble."

Chapter 13

Mo got changed carefully out of his cricket gear back into his smart clothes. He texted Rayaan who poked his head round the gates of the park and whistled. Mo told him what had happened. Rayaan looked at both of them. "You absolute idiots! Why weren't you more careful?"

Mo kicked a stone that pinged off a rubbish bin and bounced off down the path. Sammy broke the awkward silence. "Er, I better get back. I'll see you soon Mo." He half waved a goodbye then ran off quickly in the direction of his house.

Rayaan and Mo trudged back to the house in angry silence. When they arrived, they stood outside the front door for a moment. They could hear voices talking loudly. Mo put his ear to the door. He couldn't hear what was being said but he could recognise everyone – Mum, Dad and Uncle Bilal. He put his key in the lock and turned it.

Hassan darted out from the front room and pointed at the kitchen. "Mo – Mum knows you've been skipping class – Uncle Bilal came round and..."

They heard the kitchen door open and Hassan rapidly disappeared.

Bilal came out. He took a look at Mo and shook his head. Then he glowered at Rayaan and practically marched him out of the house, slamming the door behind him.

Mo walked slowly down the hall. The kitchen door was open and Mo could see Dad was standing at the door and Mum was sitting at the table. Dad looked at him.

"Come here Mo," he said.

Mo walked slowly into the room.

"We've had some very disappointing news from Bilal. He said that he saw you with Sammy on the streets when we thought you were in your Arabic class. Is that true?"

Mo said nothing.

"I said is it true?"

Mo nodded.

Now Mum chimed in. "We trusted you Mo. You gave us your word that you were going to the mosque. Instead you were running wild."

"Mum, I wasn't running wild, I was at cricket."

"I don't care where you were, you told us a lie. How can we believe you now?" Mum shook her head.

"Is that it?" asked Mo.

"Be quiet!" Dad shouted. "You've let us down
Mo. Go to your room and we'll talk about this
when Mum and I have calmed down."

Chapter 14

Calming down took quite some time.

Mo woke up on Saturday and then remembered, and wished he had stayed asleep. He stayed in bed as long as he could and Hassan sneaked him up some cereal. At about 9 o'clock he edged downstairs. There was a smell of burning in the kitchen and Dad had the toaster upside down on the table and was trying to remove a burnt crust.

"Ah, Mo," he said. "Sit down." Mum came in from the garden carrying some herbs she had just picked. She pulled up a chair and looked at him.

"This isn't really about missing Arabic class. We realise that you weren't trying to get up to mischief but you disobeyed us when we said no. There has to be trust in a family."

Mo kept his head down.

"But you've been a good boy this term – you've not been in trouble at school since Easter and we don't want to punish you too much. So we're going to ground you for a week. You can catch up on any schoolwork you need to do, entertain Hassan and help us around the house."

Mo thought this over. That wasn't too bad. Except.

"But dad, what about the final on Sunday?"

"We've decided to make an exception for that," said Mum, "you can go to the game and watch with Dad and Hassan."

"But Mum, It's the final. I'm the captain. The team *needs* me."

"I'm sorry Mo, the answer's no."

Slam.

Chapter 15

THEY'VE GROUNDED ME 😞

WHAT? WHAT ABOUT THE FINAL – U CAN STILL PLAY?

NO.

UR JOKING?

NO. THEY'VE SAID I CAN WATCH.

Chapter 16

Sunday morning, 8am. Hassan was trying to get a rolled-up pair of socks through the basketball net on the back of the bedroom door. Each time he scored, Mo threw a pillow at him.

"Get off," said Hassan chucking the pillow back. "Anyway, you need to get up, the game starts at 10."

"What's the point?"

Hassan gave him an unexpected and sympathetic hug.

Eventually, Mo pulled some clothes on, ostentatiously refused breakfast and climbed into Bilal's car with Dad and Hassan. Dad tried to jolly things along by telling a few jokes but Mo just looked out of the window, feeling glummer and glummer as they approached Sparkhill.

Everyone was already there. Mike had the team warming up outside the clubhouse, while Greystone were nearby, doing energetic fielding drills.

Dad had spoken to Mike the previous day and explained the situation. Mo sat on a bench, half playing on his phone, half watching as Mike ordered everyone to sprint round some cones. After ten minutes, Aisha and Sammy wandered over to grab some water.

"I'm sorry Mo," said Aisha, giving him a hug.

"Yeah," said Sammy, "I'm sorry too, we should have thought to go back a different way."

"It's not your fault. It's mine. Mum and Dad were always going to find out eventually." Mo kicked at a crisp packet – Aisha tutted at him and put it in the bin.

Mo nodded over at Greystone. "They look good."

Sammy nodded. "They are – you should have seen them earlier, a couple of their players can hit it miles. We'll need every run we can get."

Then he stopped and glanced at Aisha. "We'd better get back," he said.

Mo stood up slowly and turned round to look for Hassan, who was bouncing a tennis ball off the clubhouse wall. "Hey Hass, I'll bowl at you if you like?"

The boys walked off to the far side of the ground where one of the big old tree trunks could be used as stumps. Hassan clobbered Mo's first ball over his head for six. And the second. Little brothers were such a pain. Suddenly there was a scream from behind them.

They turned round to see someone on the grass clutching at his ankle. Mo rushed over. Poor Sammy was white as chalk and wincing in pain.

Mike bustled over and asked Sammy to flex his foot. Mo watched as a single tear travelled down his face. Sammy hated crying so Mo knew it must hurt. Mike stood up grim-faced. "Young man, you need to be checked up at A&E." He turned round and waved at Sammy's mum, who was already jogging over.

"I'm sorry Sammy," said Mike. "You earned your chance to play in this."

With an arm round Mo and an arm round his mum, Sammy limped to the car. He climbed in gingerly, tears still in his eyes. "I've let everyone down."

"No you haven't, Sammy – you never let anyone down." Mo watched miserably as their car disappeared round the corner.

When he turned back towards the clubhouse, Mike was waiting for him. So was his dad. Dad's hands were deep in his pockets – his thinking pose.

"Mo," called Mike, "come here a minute." Mike put his hands on his shoulders. "It's an emergency and we need you. I've spoken to your dad. He's agreed that you can play for the sake of the team."

Mo widened his eyes and gave Dad a big hug.

"Thank you so much."

Dad laughed. "You're a lucky boy."

Chapter 17

Mo ran into the changing room where the team was sitting.

"I'm in!"

"Thank god," said Aisha," I thought we'd have to go out there with ten players!"

"How did you persuade your dad?"

"I didn't," said Mo, "Mike did. But I'm so sorry for Sammy."

"I know," said Aisha. "Poor Sammy. But you know what he would want. He'd want you to go out there and win it for us." She started to pull the captaincy band from her arm.

"No," Mo said firmly. "Keep it."

Aisha smiled and stood up, hands on her hips. "Come on you lot – we need to get on the pitch."

The team filed out. Aisha had already tossed up and lost – Sparkhill were bowling first.

The Greystone openers were huge man-boys with enormous shoulders. They tore the opening attack apart. Hamza and Ben were accurate but the batters just swung through the line and heaved. Again and again Mo watched from slip as a good length ball disappeared over the boundary and into the long grass. They'd put on 102 in 11 overs before one of them finally made a mistake trying to turn a one into a two and was run out by a fine throw from deep cover.

Aisha came over to Mo as the No.3 walked in. "I'd like you to bowl now Mo, it's the right time. We need another breakthrough."

His first over was good – tight and aggressive. The new batter was on strike and feeling her way slightly. His second over went for 16 as the opener continued his onslaught with four fours. Mo stood at the end of his run and thought about poor Sammy queuing for ages at A&E with only the vending machine to keep his spirits up. Sammy would somehow keep it together, however much it hurt. He bet he'd be smiling at a nurse right now as he wiggled his leg about. So, what would Sammy say to him? Sammy would tell him to forget about the last over, and start again. Start again. Right. Here we go…

Off-break, arm ball, off-break – Howzat?! The umpire's finger went up. It was the huge opening giant, who stomped off the pitch all mammoth feet. Mo tried to look coy as the high fives came his way – it didn't work. Aisha gave him a thumbs-up but at 130 for 2, Sparkhill were still struggling.

Things didn't get much better. At the end of their 20 overs Greystone had made 172 for 5. It was a much bigger score than Sparkhill Under-13s had made all season. Now they had to better it, in the final, against the best team in the competition.

Chapter 18

The August sun was high and burning as they sat down outside the pavilion waiting to bat. Mo had already padded up, and he could feel sweat dripping down the back of his legs and pooling where the straps of his pads were tight.

Kamran and Stumpy got off to a good start in that they weren't out. But they were very slow. Mo tapped Aisha on the shoulder. "Tell them to get a move on."

"Have you seen how fast those opening bowlers are? They're doing well just to stay there."

"Yeah I know. But they have to keep the scoreboard ticking over otherwise there will be too much to do at the end."

"Howzat!?"

They turned as the fast bowler with the ginger crew cut roared an appeal. Stumpy was standing with his bum sticking out and both legs stuck in front of the stumps.

"That's out," said Mo, just as the umpire raised his finger.

"Well, there you go," said Aisha. "Your chance to show us how it's done."

Mo walked out to the middle, feeling rather sick. By luck, or rather by Sammy's bad luck, he'd been handed a chance. He had to do it for Sparkhill. He HAD to.

He asked the umpire for a middle-stump guard. He tapped his bat on the ground a couple of times to steady his nerves before looking up as the bowler got ready at the top of his mark. His muscles bulged out of his shirt. Mo thought about his own arms. "Puny," as Hassan liked to put it. But what did that matter? It was timing that counted.

The bowler charged in. Mo flashed at the first ball and it flew over first slip and down to the boundary.

"Concentrate!" came a shout. Alright Dad.

Mo played out the next few overs, nudging a few runs through the on side, edging a few more and running hard. At the other end players came and went without troubling the scorers much. It was so warm that they had a drinks break after ten overs: Sparkhill were 78 for six, needing an unlikely 94 to win.

Dylan and Mo took their helmets off and gulped down some water. Mo looked at the Greystone fielders – they were very composed. They thought they'd got this.

But suddenly Mo was seeing the ball like a balloon. The spinners came on but they were both nervous and couldn't find a steady rhythm. When they pitched it short, Mo stayed back and cut or pulled, too full and he drove powerfully. In just five overs, they put on 55. 39 needed…

There was one more over from the medium pacer. After five balls Dylan, who had played so steadily, finally lost patience. He stepped back to cut and… what was he doing?! He'd trodden on his own stumps.

As the umpires put the leg stump back upright, Mo did some mental calculations. With three wickets, and four overs left, they still needed 33.

Aisha strode in as if she was on her way to the ice-cream parlour to pick up a double cone with raspberry sauce. "Are we winning this?" she asked through the grille of her helmet.

"Er…"

"Wrong answer. Come on!"

She positioned herself at the non-striker's end, as Greystone brought back the heavy mob. "Breathe," Mo said to himself as he watched the two fast bowlers limber up.

The slightly slimmer bowler took the ball. His first two deliveries were wides, which Mo left alone. The bowler was visibly nervous and Mo saw the long hop coming, rocked onto his back foot and pulled it to the boundary. They hit another 6 runs from the over – 21 more needed.

Ginger was incredibly calm. And incredibly fast. Somehow Mo and Aisha cobbled together four singles. His heart was hammering so hard, he thought his chest might burst open. From the middle he could hear Hassan chanting and see Dad, pacing up and down, up and down.

With 12 balls left Aisha was on strike. She swung and missed at the first ball. And then the second. They scrambled a run from the third, then Mo flicked a couple of fours off his legs. They needed a single off the last ball so Mo could face the final over. The ball was on a good length and Mo scuffed it up towards point. He called Aisha through for a run but as he sprinted up the pitch he watched in horror as the extra-cover fielder came across, threw himself at the ball and hurled it at the wicket-keeper. Aisha was run out by half a metre. As Greystone celebrated, Mo kicked the ground in frustration. They needed eight from Ginger's final over, with only Adi and Charlie left to bat. And even on their best days they held the bat as if it was a pair of dirty socks they'd just pulled out from under the bed.

By the time Adi arrived in the middle, he was green. "Let's just have some fun," said Mo, trying to look upbeat. "I'm Babar Azam and you're Imam-ul-Haq in that run-chase against Australia."

Adi was sceptical. "Mo, my highest score is three. Also, I can't get out because Charlie is being sick in the dressing-room."

Ginger was at the top of his mark. He took one step, two, and started to speed up.

Chapter 19

Mo went back to basics. He kept his head steady, his bat hovering by his ankles. He breathed in and out as he watched Ginger's feet thundering towards him. Ginger reached the stumps, and... whoosh... the ball passed by Mo's bat.

There was a cheer from the wicket-keeper. "Keep it up, Ginger."

Mo closed his eyes and refocused. He stretched down and touched his toes. Ginger was ready to go again. He released a bullet on his legs – but Mo saw it early, and clipped it away to the boundary.

Adi came down, his eyes wide with excitement. "Four needed Mo, four balls left."

The next delivery was a repeat of the first one, only faster, and Mo couldn't get bat on it. There was now a huddle between the Greystone captain, Ginger and the wicket-keeper. Mo kept his eye on the field changes, and whipped the next ball off his toes. He'd just turned for the second run and was half way down the pitch when he noticed that Adi had slipped and was on his bottom. Mo scrambled back to the non-striker's end and just beat the fielder's throw. They were safe but Adi was facing! He had to get down the other end.

Ginger ran in. It was a yorker, which Adi somehow kept out. The ball squirted towards mid-wicket and Mo charged down the pitch and threw himself at the stumps, landing as elegantly as a chest of drawers thrown on a tip, just beating the ball home.

He stood up and dusted himself off, trousers filthy and torn. On the boundary he could see the whole of Sparkhill bouncing up and down with excitement and Mike standing with arms firmly folded across his chest.

Greystone arranged and rearranged the field. "What are you going to do, Mo?" asked Adi. "A boundary would do it."

Mo rolled his eyes before putting his helmet back on. "Thanks for the advice."

He took a moment to check the field – a ring around him and then four on the buondary. Hmmmm. He looked at Ginger – where was he going to bowl it? Full probably. Yes, he would try a yorker.

Mo stood as still as he'd ever stood, then, as Ginger released the ball, he shuffled square, kept his bat straight and flicked the ball over his left shoulder. The most perfect, beautiful scoop shot. It soared over the wicket-keeper and flew to the boundary rope.

They'd done it! Mo and Adi threw their arms around each other. In seconds, the rest of the team had reached them, hollering and whooping. Mo let himself be jumped all over, eventually pulling himself from the bottom of the pile when Aisha reminded them, with a huge grin, that they needed to shake hands with the opposition.

Mo turned to find that Greystone had lined up at the side of the pitch and were waiting for them. "That's proper," Aisha whispered.

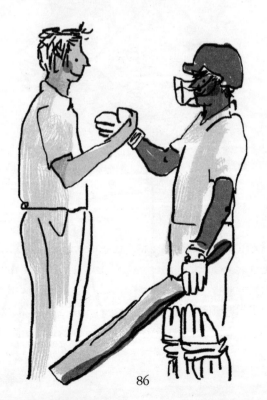

Mo shook hands with each of them in turn from the gigantic opening batters to Ginger, who folded Mo's hand in his and said, "Well played, that was awesome." Mo beamed. "Thanks. You didn't do too bad yourself."

A little further back Dad was waiting with Hassan, who knocked him to the ground in a huge brotherly wrestle-hug. Dad shook his hand, and Mum gave him a squeeze. "Dad phoned me," she said. "You were brilliant."

From somewhere drinks, crisps and ice-lollies appeared and no-one was in a hurry to go home. By mid-afternoon, a giant game of soft-ball cricket had taken over half the outfield. Some families from the estate wandered over and joined in, including Mina, whose cousin, it turned out, played for Greystone.

Mo had retreated to the shade to sit with Mum and Dad when Mike came over. He squatted down next to them. "Mo, you played so well today – such a mature performance. If you can keep that standard up next year, we'll have Warwickshire knocking on our door." He stood up and cleared his throat.

"Also, I wish you'd come to talk to me about the problems you had with practice on a Thursday. I'm not an ogre, I'd have made allowances."

Mo looked up. "Thanks."

Mike nodded gruffly and left.

"Is that Mike being emotional?" asked Hassan.

"Shhh," said Mum laughing. "But, he's right. You've got a god-given talent, perhaps we should have been more flexible too."

Dad nodded enthusiastically. "If he wants to be a cricketer, he has to practise all he can."

Mum was talking about the importance of schoolwork but Mo was zoning out. *If* he wanted to be a cricketer... *of course* he wanted to be a cricketer. This was just the beginning. Today Sparkhill, tomorrow Warwickshire... His phone pinged. It was Sammy:

"ANKLE NOT BROKEN. SEVERE SPRAIN – REST AND CHOCOLATE NEEDED.

PS: YOU ABSOLUTE LEGEND!"

The Legend of Sparkhill, yes that had a ring to it. He closed his eyes and lay down. Life was suddenly getting a lot more interesting.

Acknowledgments

Huge thanks to Kamran Abbasi, Charlie Campbell, Hamza Jahanzeb, Umran Khan, Zulekha Olia-Khan, Saj Sadiq and Matt Thacker; to Andy, Rosy, Sonny and Dylan for their good-humoured encouragement; and most of all to Moeen Ali, for being an all-round superstar.

About the authors

Tanya Aldred

Tanya Aldred has written about cricket for 25 years, for all sorts of publications but mostly the *Guardian*. She also runs creative writing classes for children alongside her journalism.

Moeen Ali OBE

Moeen Ali is one of the world's most popular and iconic cricketers. He has played red and white ball cricket for England, captaining the side four times as well as leading Worcestershire and Birmingham Phoenix. In 2021 he won the IPL playing for Chennai Super Kings. Off the field, he is a thoughtful and influential figure, writing an occasional column for the *Guardian*. He was named one of *Wisden*'s five cricketers of the year in 2015 and his autobiography was shortlisted for the *Telegraph* Sports Book Awards and longlisted for the National Book Awards. He was awarded the OBE in the Queen's Platinum Jubilee Honours list for services to cricket.

Proceeds from the book

The authors and publishers have agreed that at least 30% of any profits that *The Legend of Sparkhill* generates will be donated to Chance to Shine. In addition, profits from the book will help one talented young boy or girl from the area where Mo grew up on their journey towards County Age Cricket.

About Chance to Shine

Chance to Shine is a national charity on a mission to spread the power of cricket throughout schools and communities. The charity takes cricket to new places and uses it to ignite new passions, teach vital skills, unite diverse groups, and educate young people across the UK. Find out more at *chancetoshine.org*.

About the National Asian Cricket Council

The National Asian Cricket Council exists to support and promote the interests of the South Asian Cricketing Community at national and regional levels, whilst developing positive relationships between key stakeholders such as the England and Wales Cricket Board (ECB), County Boards and their immediate cricketing communities.

Over 30 per cent of recreational cricket players are from the south Asian cricketing community, but representation at first-class level is still only around the five per cent mark.